For all those who have been, and continue to be, touched by dementia. Especially our very wonderful Veronica Spry
— C H W

For my Granny Teasie and Barbara Anne
— A L

LITTLE TIGER PRESS LTD,
an imprint of the Little Tiger Group
1 Coda Studios, 189 Munster Road, London SW6 6AW
www.littletiger.co.uk

First published in Great Britain 2019

A CIP catalogue record for this book is available from the British Library

 • ISBN 978-1-78881-085-2
Printed in China • LTP/1400/2415/0918

2 4 6 8 10 9 7 5 3 1

The Tide

Clare Helen Welsh

Ashling Lindsay

LITTLE TIGER

LONDON

Sometimes Grandad forgets things.
Like he did the day we set up camp and
watched the tide come in.

Mummy says that Grandad loves me very much but that sometimes he gets confused.

She says it must be annoying to forget how to do things and I agree.

Like the time I couldn't
remember how to put my shoes on
and my teacher helped me.

So when we're at the beach,
I hold Grandad's hand.

We sculpture forts and castles.

We are the king and queen of
net and shells . . .
and we watch the tide come in.

We picnic in the sun . . .

but where are all the sandwiches?

I love my grandad but sometimes I get cross when he does odd things.

I try to remember it must be scary to forget.

Like the time I
buried Polar Bear
and Mummy helped
me find him.

So when we're at the beach, I give
Grandad a big kiss.

We search for sleepy starfish.
We jump from pool to pool . . .

and we watch the
tide come in.

But what if Grandad forgets ME?

It must be frightening to forget someone you love.
I haven't ever forgotten somebody that important.

Mummy says Grandad's memories are like the tide.
Sometimes near and close and full of life.

Other times, far away and distant.

But I know that he loves me more
than lapping waves and sandy toes
on sunny days.

All of a sudden, we hear voices!
Happy, laughing voices from
around the next cove;
everybody smiles.

But Grandad's smile is the biggest.
We gather our coins and pennies.
We savour every lick . . .

and we watch the tide.

But the tide is in!

We dip our startled toes. We dance through rolling waves.
Because the tide is in!

We shower in the spray. We wave at smiling gulls.
Because the tide is in!

Then we empty out our pockets,
and dry our sandy clothes.

We wash our salty skin,
then snuggle nice and close . . .

. . . to talk about the day we
watched the tide come in.

Because Grandad doesn't remember
things like he used to.

But I love him as much as I always have.
And I know that he loves me.